Dingle's Christmas Adventure

By Peter Simon

Illustrations by Paula Lawson

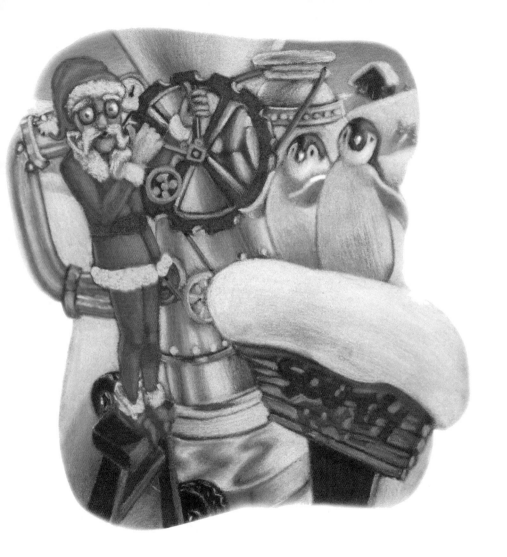

Not many people know Santa Claus has a younger brother named Dingle, who lives at the South Pole where he works as an inventor.

Dingle Claus has invented many things, including a glacier cube'o'rake, a snow coniker and hoof heaters to keep reindeers' hooves warm.

2

Dingle has not sold many of his inventions.

He is also clumsy, and he likes carrots better than cookies.

4

One day a few years ago around Christmas time Dingle called his brother. "Hello, Claudette Claus speaking," said Mrs. Claus, because saying your name when you answer the phone is polite.

"Hi Claudette." said Dingle. "Oh! Oh! Oh! How are things at the North Pole?"

"Oh dear. Santa's sick with Pole Fever. I don't think he's going to get better in time to deliver toys to all the good girls and boys," replied Claudette.

"I'll come and help you!" hooted Dingle.

" Well..." said Mrs. Claus.

But Dingle was already packing.

"Oh, Oh, Oooh," said
Dingle to himself.
"Somebody's got to help
and that 'somebody'
might as well be me!"

He jumped on the Polevator that runs through the center of the earth from the South Pole to the North Pole.

He pressed the "Up" button and lied down to take a nap, because the Polevator ride takes a long time.

"Santa, Dingle is on his way here to deliver the toys for you," said Mrs. Claus. Santa's face looked like he had seen a house without a chimney.

"My brother cannot deliver Christmas toys all over the world in one night," muttered Santa. "He's clumsy and forgetful and does not know how to drive the reindeer."

"But he is a clever inventor," said Claudette. Surely you can teach him what to do?"

"Maybe. I suppose he should be here, just in case," replied Santa.

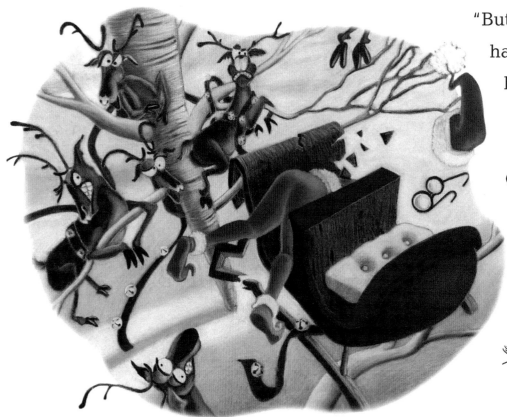

"But remember what happened the last time he was here."

"Yes, that was unfortunate," said Claudette. "Here, I've made you some pine needle tea."

10

Santa sipped his tea
while snow swirled
outside and the fire
burned brightly.

Before you
could whisper,
"On Dasher, on Dancer!"
they fell asleep.

Dingle burst into
the living room a
few hours later,
fresh as a
brand new
snowfall from
his nap in
the Polevator.
"Oh Oh Oh!"
he yelled.
Santa and Claudette
jumped awake like somebody
had just yelled, "Oh Oh Oh!"
Then the doorbell rang.
"Now who could that be?" wondered Mrs. Claus.

12

She opened the door. There stood
Horatio, the elf in charge
of Santa's workshop.
"I'm sorry to bother
you, but we have
a challenge,"
Horatio said.
"The marble-making
machine got jammed
with thousands of
marbles stuck inside."
"I can fix that," said
Dingle cheerfully.
"Oh hi, Dingle,"
said Horatio nervously.

He remembered the last time Dingle
tried to help out in the workshop.
"Let's go have a look," said Dingle.

14

Dingle poked at the marble-making machine.

"Horatio, do you have a flibberdeejibbit?"

"Coming right up."

Dingle fiddled with the flibberdeejibbit, and suddenly...

...the marble machine burst open!

"Dingle! Now look what you've done!" cried Horatio. He pulled the workshop alarm and all the elves stood perfectly still.

The flood of marbles finally stopped rolling.

"I have an idea," Dingle whispered.

"We'll take care of this ourselves!" exclaimed Horatio.

Dingle left and came back with his glacier cube'o'rake. He had all the marbles back in the machine faster than Santa gobbles down a plate of cookies.

"Thank you," grumbled Horatio grudgingly. "You're welcome," replied Dingle. "Oh, Oh, Oh!

Santa took Dingle into his Christmas delivery room later that night. He showed his brother the secrets of how to drive the sleigh and deliver the toys all over the world in a single night.

"I'm worried about whether Dingle can do the job," Santa said wearily as he climbed into bed. "He means well, but he made a lot of mistakes while I was trying to teach him." "People will often surprise you when you give them a chance to prove what they can do," said Mrs. Claus. "I hope you're right," sighed Santa. They went to sleep and dreamed of sugarplums all night long.

The next night was Christmas Eve.
The elves loaded the sleigh,
while Santa watched from his
bedroom window.
The time came to go.
Santa ran wheezing out
of the house.
"Wait! I can
do this,"
he gasped.
"Dingle, please
get down."

Santa tried to
get into the
sleigh, but he
was too weak
from Pole Fever
to climb aboard.

Santa William Claus, what in the name of Rudolph do you

think you're doing?" Claudette scolded. "Please let Dingle help us."

You are too sick to do your job," said Dingle.

You have shown me well how to drive the sleigh

and deliver the toys.

Let me get out

there and deliver

these toys,

Dingle-style!"

Oh, very well,"

grumbled Santa.

Call me if you

have any questions."

Dingle climbed back aboard, grabbed the reins and yelled, "Now, Dasher! Now, Dancer! Now, Prancer and Vixen! On, Comet! On, Cupid! On, Donder and Blitzen!" The reindeer did not move. Dingle hollered their names again, louder.

The reindeer looked back and shook their antlers.

Santa threw open his bedroom
window and yelled, "Giddyap!"

The reindeer took off like a jet,
whisking Dingle and the sleigh
into the night sky.

"Forgot to tell him that part,"
mumbled Santa.

Dingle and the reindeers landed roughly on the first roof. Dingle delivered the toys in a flash and came back to the sleigh.

"Giddyap!" he yelled.

The reindeer tried to scramble to their feet, but the icy roof was too slippery.

"Uh oh!" said Dingle. "What in the name of stocking stuffers am I going to do?"

"Ah ha!"

Dingle opened the trur of the sleigh and pulle out the hoof heaters.

Moments
later, they
were back
in the sky.

Dingle dangled his way

through a few houses...

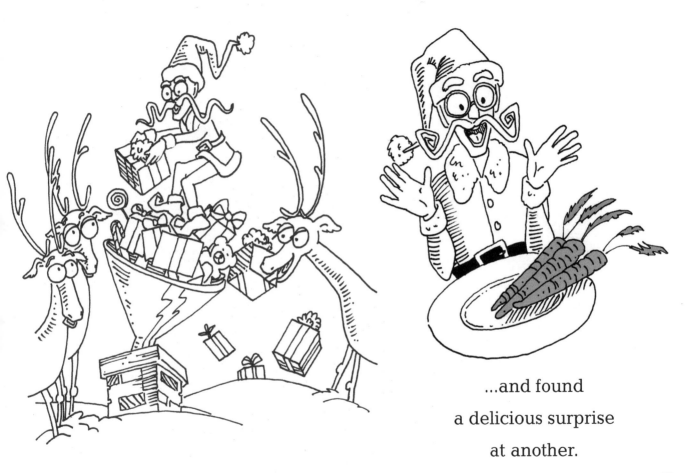

...and found

a delicious surprise

at another.

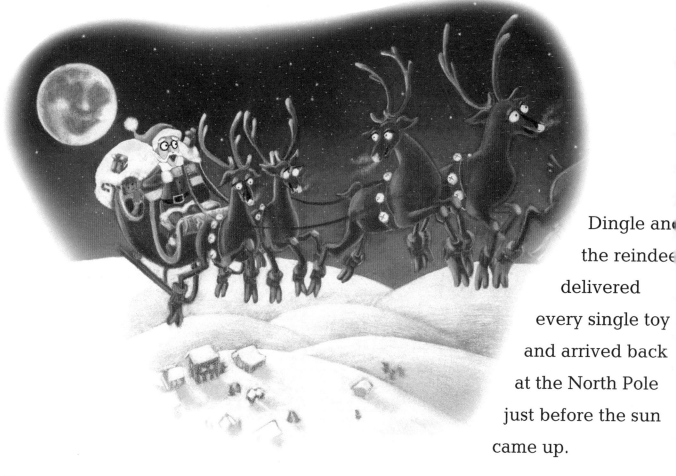

Dingle and
the reindeer
delivered
every single toy
and arrived back
at the North Pole
just before the sun
came up.

The elves cheered wildly.
Mrs. Claus hugged
Dingle and Santa
danced a jig.

Even the reindeer
nuzzled Dingle,
though Donder and
Blitzen kept trying
to take off their hoof heaters.

"Thank you, brother," said Santa.

"You're welcome," replied Dingle.
"But I did not do this alone. You taught me well and the elves made the toys
and the reindeer flew in bad weather and Claudette's pine needle tea kept me
warm all night. We delivered Christmas together! Now why don't we
take the Polevator to my house and celebrate?"

So they did.

The End

A note for those reading aloud to children: "Dingle's Christmas Adventure" features learning moments for you to discuss with your listener(s). Dingle and his friends demonstrate resilience, creativity, and perseverance, valuable characteristics in our friends, family, and ourselves! How can we use our different strengths to make the world a better place? How is teamwork important in Dingle's story, and in our own lives? Many hands make light work. I hope you enjoy sharing "Dingle's Christmas Adventure" as much as I enjoyed writing the story. Happy reading! – Peter Simon

47352193R00022